This book belongs to:

....

....

For my four favourite children
in the whole wide world,
Elliott, Scarlet, Gabby and Annie
– Steve Smallman

Editor: Ruth Symons
Designer: Krina Patel
Editorial Director: Victoria Garrard
Art Director: Laura Roberts-Jensen

Copyright © QED Publishing 2014

First published in the UK in 2014 by QED Publishing
A Quarto Group company, The Old Brewery, 6 Blundell Street, London, N7 9BH

www.qed-publishing.co.uk

A catalogue record for this book is available from the British Library.

ISBN 978 1 78171 573 4

Printed in China

BATMOUSE

Steve Smallman

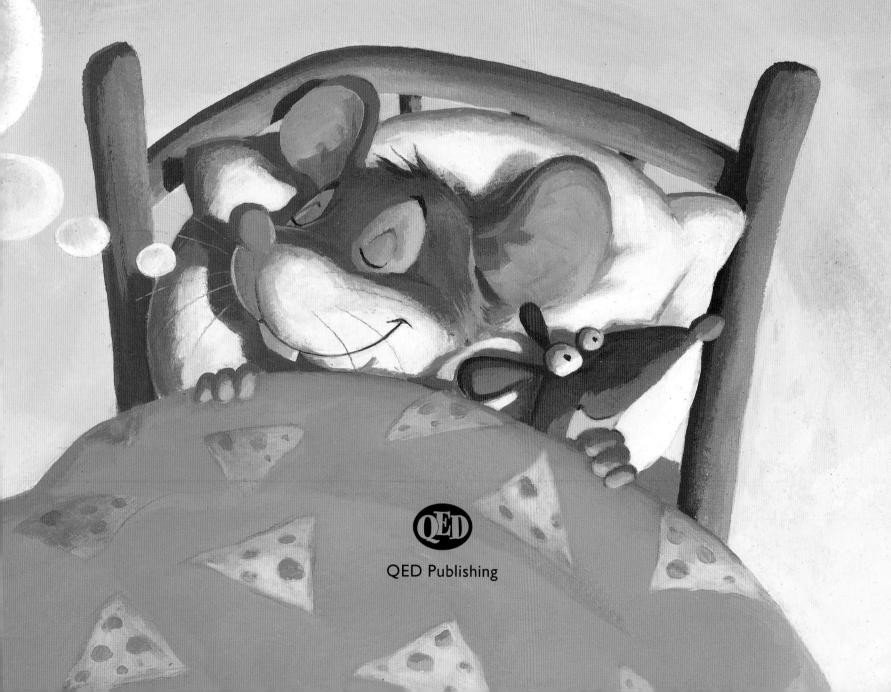

QED Publishing

Squeeeeeeak!

"Look Mum," said Pip,
"it's a flying mouse!"

"That's not a mouse,"
said Mum. "It's a bat."

"I wish I could fly," said Pip.
"When I grow up, can I be a bat?"

"You can't be a bat," said Mum.
"Look — you don't have any wings."

So Pip made some wings out of an
old cardboard box. Soon he was
ready for take-off!

"Look Mum, I'm a batmouse!"

Pip rushed around, squeaking his squeakiest
squeak and flapping his cardboard wings up
and down. But he just couldn't fly.

So he tried again...

...and again...

...and again!

He flapped till he flopped,
tired and dizzy on the floor.

"Never mind Pip," said Mum.
To cheer him up, she made his favourite supper
— stinky cheese and biscuit crumbs.

At bedtime, Pip couldn't get comfortable.
His wings kept getting caught in the covers.

"That's because bats
hang upside down
when they sleep,"
said Mum.

Pip tried lying upside down.
But he still wasn't comfortable.

The next morning, Pip climbed
up to the top of Windy Hill.

"Time to fly!" he squeaked,
flapping his wings as hard as
he could. Pip jumped!

BUMP!

He landed on his bottom
and rolled, over and
over and over, all the
way down the hill.

Pip's head was spinning,
his bottom was bruised and his
wings were all tattered and torn.

Then he heard a familiar sound...

Squeeeeeak!

It was coming from inside a little cave.
The cave was dark and spooky,
but Pip tried to be brave.

"H...h...hello?"

he squeaked.

"Hello," said an upside down voice. "I'm Albert. Who are you?"

"I'm P...P...P...Pip, and I'm a batmouse!"

"Really?" asked Albert. "But you seem to be the wrong way up."

"Oops, sorry!" said Pip, and he stood on his head.

"Your wings look a bit... cardboardy,"
said Albert.

"My real wings haven't
grown yet!" said Pip.

"Ah, that explains it," said Albert with a smile.
"Well, little batmouse, are you hungry?"
Pip was VERY hungry.

"Have you got any stinky cheese?" he asked.

"Stinky cheese!" cried Albert. "Bats don't eat stinky cheese! How about a nice juicy moth?"

Pip looked at the moth
and burst into tears.

"I'M NOT A
BATMOUSE!"

he blurted.

"I DON'T WANT TO LIVE IN A SPOOKY CAVE,

OR EAT MOFFS,

OR HANG UPSIDE DOWN...

...BUT I REALLY, REALLY WANT TO FLY!"

"Then fly with me!" said Albert. "Just this once."

He picked Pip up, and carried him
out into the twinkly, twilight sky.

They soared over Windy Hill, through the treetops

and finally landed right outside Pip's house.

"Well, little batmouse," whispered
Albert, "do you like flying?"

"I think so," said Pip, who felt dizzy and scared
and excited all at once. "Thank you, Albert."

As Albert fluttered away, Pip spotted a big pile of earth. First a nose, and then two feet pushed their way above the ground.

"LOOK MUM,"
Pip cried.
"It's a DIGGING MOUSE!"

"That's not a mouse, Pip, it's a mole," said Mum.
"When I grow up, can I be a mole?" asked Pip.

"Here we go again..." sighed Mum.

NEXT STEPS

Show the children the cover again. Could they have guessed what the story was about just from looking at the cover? Did any of the children think it would be a superhero story?

Pip really wanted to be a bat. Ask the children which animal they would like to be and why. How would they make themselves look like that animal?

Pip tried very hard to look and act like a bat. Can the children remember all the things he did?

Ask the children if they would like to fly. What would they see if they flew over their home? How would they feel?

Did Pip enjoy pretending to be a bat? Ask the children if they have ever wanted something, then been disappointed when they finally got it.

Pip likes eating stinky cheese and biscuit crumbs. Albert likes eating moths. Ask the children if they would like to eat stinky cheese. What is their favourite food? Talk about how different people like different things.

Ask the children what Pip wants to be at the end of the story. What do they think he will do to make himself more like this animal?